Remember to Forget

A novella

Remember to Forget

A novella

Jonny Gibbings

PERFECT
EDGE
BOOKS

Winchester, UK
Washington, USA

First published by Perfect Edge Books, 2014

Perfect Edge Books is an imprint of John Hunt Publishing Ltd., Laurel House, Station Approach, Alresford, Hants, SO24 9JH, UK

office1@jhpbooks.net

www.johnhuntpublishing.com

www.perfectedgebooks.com

For distributor details and how to order please visit the 'Ordering' section on our website.

ISBN: 978 1 78279 388 5

A CIP catalogue record for this book is available from the British Library.

Design: Stuart Davies
www.stuartdaviesart.com

Printed in the USA by Edwards Brothers Malloy

We operate a distinctive and ethical publishing philosophy in all areas of our business, from our global network of authors to production and worldwide distribution.

Acknowledgements

To the fathers that are dads and to the mums that give love unconditional, when your children become adults they will know who real superheroes are. To the boys and girls like me, who grew into adults never knowing this love, we can be heroes too. To Sophie, a true warrior woman, Kai and Ella for the gift that they are, thank you. If you stick with it, love always wins.

AND.

'And' is a word that shouldn't be able to cause such pain, it is a functional word not a provocative one. There are so many words that could be loaded with the bullets of hatred or ignorance or bigotry that would never be directed at him, delivered with such potency that they could penetrate his thick hubristic skin. Yet the ones he did qualify for, what hatred he warranted, he had defended against with vainglorious armour hewn from a life he now knew to have been selfish. A fact that was every bit a revaluation. Hindsight, he thought, was a pointless and painful endeavour, in much the same way as truth is. They say, 'With the benefit of hindsight.' The only benefit he knew of that resulted from hindsight was the knowledge of what was done was already done. Unlike the truth. Truth was like air, it surrounded him, and so he hid from it in a vacuum and slowly suffocated.

He knew Anna was in the room due to her perfume. It clung to the air, sweet and floral, yet exotic. It triggered a distant memory that seemed to not want to reveal itself, of a long ago time on far away shores. Under any other circumstance he might have smiled, let a crease creep across his mouth and announce pleasure. But he knew his wife Anna wasn't wearing perfume for him, it was for Robert. He didn't know who Robert was, but he seemed to make her happy, he made her laugh. Richard was like a child that has walked in halfway through a movie, he had no point of reference as to how long this affair or fling or love or whatever it was called had existed. The only time he would hear Anna's voice was when she was on the phone to him. Once she was embarrassed to take the calls, it wasn't decent to conduct herself in such a way in front of him, Anna always was classy like that. But now she did.

She discussed post-him plans, of a future and its arrangements, of them staying at her hotel and soon the flat, and when it got sexual, she would speak in low hushed tones, embarrassed and accented by a uniquely abashed laugh. He knew this, because he knew this.

The exception to this was of course her monosyllabic responses to the nurses. Usually 'Thanks' or 'Okay'. Or when trying to instil some semblance of the seriousness of the situation to her errant daughter, who like her mother, scheduled ever-waning visits due to being obligated to appear to care. Presumably only to each other.

"Ella, for Christ sake, what do you mean you won't be able to visit for a couple of weeks? You've seen your father for an hour at best."

"I'm going to Kavos," she said with defiance, placing a clutch of large boutique shopping bags on the floor.

"Ella," Anna pleaded. "You do realise your father might very well die this week?"

"*And*?"

The heaviness of the small, empty word worried little about his armour, overwhelmingly crushing him as it fell from his daughter's lips. He was a vessel, his family his cargo that he selfishly sailed into oceans of isolation and regret only to foolishly run aground. His family now waited on the shore for him to sink from view so they could profit from what flotsam and jetsam would wash ashore. He wanted to open his eyes and look upon his wife. She was the star he once navigated by. He wasn't foolish, he knew just as all stars, what he saw and what is, were not the same. The distance between him and his star so vast that the love that once shone so bright died so very long ago. Even if he were able to open his eyes they were taped down to protect them from drying out. Not something he needed to fear now. Two tiny globes of tear formed in the cusp of each eye, and rivered down his cheeks.

Silence quickly filled the void in the room, what wasn't said so much more painful than any words that could have been weaponised and used. Anger he could cope with, but nothing? No response. At best he was an inconvenience.

They were both still there in the room. He could hear the gentle tap of lacquered acrylic nail upon smartphone and the digital notification that whomever Ella was talking to had replied. He imagined 'SOZ not ded yet lolz' being typed. He could hear Anna rubbing cream into her dry ageing hands that protested with a whispering rasp as she tried to erase evidence of liver spots. He could hear perfectly well. They didn't know that, nobody did; but he heard everything.

The nurses spoke to him for a time. They would say 'Morning, Richard, how are we?' Or 'Can you hear me, Richard?' They would ask and engage him as if he were still the person that he once was as they fluffed pillows, took blood, applied a clip to his finger to register heart rates. Over weeks Richard became Mr Price. Now they addressed him in the indefinite, 'the patient', almost existing in past tense as they readied Anna progressively for bad news.

Except for one nurse who sang each attendance of joy and hope. She had what he believed was a Caribbean or Jamaican accent, he wasn't sure though if they meant the same thing. She smelt of biscuits and when she walked her feet slapped the floor as if her legs were accidentally too long or the floor simply surprisingly nearer than she expected. He imagined her overweight, in slippers, like the black woman in the Tom and Jerry cartoons, seeing her illustrated only from the calf down and in red slippers. He worried if thinking as such was racist. He had spent far too long thinking about what to be rather than who he was, to have previously suffered such dilemmas.

He heard the nurses' intimate conversations, grievances with work, heard when the breakfast and lunch trolleys arrived. He heard the cleaners, the porters and how the nurses spoke differently to people when doctors were doing their rounds. He heard everything. His hearing registered as brain activity on CT scans and was the one thing keeping the machines on continuing his life. He knew this, because Dr. Raul told his wife, who said, "That is fantastic news."

As soon as the doctor had left, she growled, "Hurry up and die, you old bastard."

He had been ready to die, happy to go in fact, knowing he had provided for a family and that they were cared for, right up to where they accidentally informed him that he hadn't.

He couldn't sink yet. He had to find some way to swim to shore and build them a raft of salvage and sail them to safer waters, away from the bleak and barren wastes he had beached them upon. Except that he couldn't.

He wished they could hear him, hear him say sorry. To tell them now was their time to blossom. But he couldn't. Denied even the ability to physically manifest his anger and grief, *God, I wish someone could hear me,* he wished.

'I can hear you,' a voice said.

Richard lay silent. For all the many weeks he lay prone, mania had set in, he was sure of this. What little grasp on reality existed in his black world had more suffered a tectonic shift than a slip. He could hear his daughter sigh. Smell Anna and feel some third party busy with the chart at the bottom of his bed.

'Hello?' he said.

'Hello,' the voice replied.

'You can you hear me?'

'Yes.'

'Am I imagining this?'

'No.'

'Prove it,' Richard said, believing solely in his doubt.

'No.'

'Then I don't believe you're real.'

'Okay.'

'What the fuck do you mean okay? It doesn't bother you that I don't believe you?'

'No.'

The darkness seemed limitless, where thoughts and regrets collected along a sluice of reminiscental loathing. The longer he spent prone the longer he had to harvest memories and for them to now spill everywhere due to the intrusion of an unexpected voice. A voice not in any way intimidated by him, and this too was an alien concept. 'Fine, I will ignore you then.'

'Okay.'

Stubbornness abandoned Richard, he couldn't fill the space with silence for very long. His mind was all he had left and he feared he was losing it, he was lost to grief. 'Please,' he begged. He realised even his thoughts were shouting, he imagined speaking softly as he thought, 'If you are real, *please* show me.'

'Okay,' the voice said.

'What do you mean okay?' There was no answer. 'Hello?' Richard resigned to the sullen belief that the voice was indeed imagined and that he was indeed losing his mind.

Time now uncalendared, everything painfully slow once in the situation where you simply exist, waiting for an ending. When the voice spoke, it was after a punishingly long time.

'The next voice you will hear will be your daughter. She

will sigh. Once done replying to her friend on her phone, she will say to Anna, your wife, that she has to go. She will call Anna "Mother", not "Mum", such is the detachment you burdened your family with. Anna will ask her to think about what she said. Ella, your daughter will reply, "All I am thinking of is Kavos" and will then leave.'

'Oh god,' Richard thought. 'I hope you are a cruel imagination, please don't be real.'

'Why?' the voice asked.

'Because I would rather go mad, lose my mind than know my daughter thought that little of me. Please, I beg you, don't be real.'

'I'm sorry,' the voice said.

Ella sighed. Her long bejewelled nails danced across the glass screen of her phone as a message was composed then sent. "Mother, I've got to go."

"Ella," Anna chided sternly, "you should think about what I said."

"All I am thinking about is Kavos," she replied, collecting her bags and leaving.

Richard was consumed by the agony of bereavement, because he loved her. He loved his daughter so much. He hated the isolation and disunion he had infected his family with like a disease. He called out childhood names, 'Pinkie' and 'Minxie-may' but to no avail as the wailing existed only in his mind. Not long after his daughter left Anna followed so she wouldn't appear to be the one who didn't care. Leaving Richard alone and adrift. Clinging to weathered timbers, sinking slowly, aided by the dark truths so heavy they were a big black anvil that lay in his thought and would drown him further amongst the wreckage of his life. The silence that followed an eternity uncounted.

'It's okay,' the voice finally spoke.

'No, it isn't.'

'Okay,' it said.

'How can you hear me?' he asked.

'Because.'

'Are you what I think you are?'

'Yes.'

'An angel?'

'No.'

'So you are *not* what I thought you were?' Richard thought.

'I am. But the term you use is a manmade one. Angel, is is a label made of men, there is no such thing.'

Richard thought carefully how he would ask his next question. After much consternation about phrasing the question to provide a more favourable if less honest answer, Richard decided it was the blunt brittle truth he needed. 'Am I going to die?'

'Yes.'

The answer as cold as the chronicle of disengagement that he had written in ink of ostentation. The loss of his family greater than that of his own passing. 'Will you help me?' he thought.

'How?'

'I don't want to die.'

'Well, you are.'

'Can you buy me some time?'

'Buy? Your money holds no value to me, Richard.'

'That's not what I meant. Could you *give* me more time?'

'As a gift?'

'If that is what it would be, I need time.'

'Why?'

'To fix things.'

'Why?'

'Because I can't leave my family like this. They don't...'

'They don't what?'

'Fit together, my family is broken. It's my fault isn't it?'

'Yes.'

'How? I gave them everything they ever wanted. I worked my ass off to provide them with wonderful things, so how did this happen?'

'You gave them everything *you* wanted. You never listened to what they wanted. You worked hard because you wanted to win, not to provide.'

'I need time to try and make things better. I can't leave a daughter who is so cold she doesn't care if her father dies and a son who cares even less. I know I am going to die, I'm not asking for me, it's for them, my family, I need to...' He hated the admission that he was to blame, he struggled to offer up the words to beg with.

'To what?' the voice asked.

'Repair what I've made, because it's my fault. Am I too late?'

'For them or for you?'

'Them.'

'I don't think so, there is time.'

'Can you help me? I'm begging you.'

'I will try.'

'What do you mean "try"? Can't you do godly doings and just make it so?'

'No. I have to ask. We are not so different to you, we have people we are answerable to. Bosses if you will. There is a balance, there are weights and measures, checks and balances that need to be applied. But I will ask.'

'Thank you.'

'You don't have to thank me.'

'What do I call you?' Richard asked.

'I am called many things.'

'Do you have a name?'

'I have many names, Michael, Gabriel, Samael, Yama,

Azrael, take your pick.'

'Gabriel?'

'If you wish. Richard, I am going to seek the answer to your question, if I might help you. You must do the same, because if so, you will not have much time. I need you to understand what the problem is to fix it.'

'I do.'

'No, you don't. You see it but you don't understand it. They are two very different things.'

'I don't know what that means.'

'Then I cannot help you.'

'If you were to help me, you would show me what that means. I'm asking for help, not for you to fix everything.'

'Okay.'

'Okay you will help or okay you won't?' Silence returned. 'Gabriel?'

* * *

Richard slept in a matryoshka doll of other sleeps, such was the world of being in a coma. There was awake-sleep, sleep-sleep and the hours of mindless numb, that was not unlike the place you go to when in a daydream that was a cul-de-sac of thoughts, but unable to escape. Early nurses didn't bother with the bother of him, just a cursory glance at his outputs. Richard was thought of as more taking up space than a patient, and one that the machines simply prolonged the inevitable outcome of and his wife didn't care too much about. Had the nurse checked the brain output or printed its receipt, she would have seen activity reminiscent of the measurement of an earthquake. When exhaustion hadn't fed sleep, Richard was at a loss as to his conversation with the voice. Was it a dream or was it simply his own reconciliation of how over time he had bullied his family into becoming emotionally disabled? Sense and reason informed him the voice couldn't have been real just as the tooth fairy wasn't, but he had never wished more in his life for reason to be wrong.

'Richard, open your eyes,' the voice said.

'Thank God, I thought I imagined you.'

'Open your eyes.'

'I can't, they are taped down.'

'Your tears have moistened the tape. The light will hurt for a while, but it will get better quickly so don't worry. Open your eyes.'

Richard felt the tension lift as the adhesive let go and his eyes opened, only to slam shut. The light was like fire. Squinting, he blinked. The small room pulled into focus, smaller than he imagined. Tattier too. He could see the age on the door frame, a piece of the laminate missing from the cabinet beside his bed, the curtains shielding from the grey outside faded somewhat. The observations brought a deep joy. He tried to speak but the endotracheal tube denied him his words. 'Thank you,' he thought.

'Richard, look at your bedside cabinet. What do you see?' Atrophy made it difficult to turn, as did the thick hose that coiled into his person, but could not resist the freedom of his eyes. Upon the cabinet sat a framed picture of a little boy, four years old, excavating a hole in the wet sea sand. A beaming smile through a zinc-white slathered face. More sand in his hair than in his bucket. Anna was behind, cut-off jeans unbuttoned and unzipped as they struggled to contain the baby weight that once packaged a baby now nestled in his arms. He was still slim. He and Anna were laughing. He recalled the day clearly, joy radiated from the memory. 'A picture,' Richard replied.

'It isn't just a picture, Richard. What is the picture?'

'My family.'

'Not who, what?' the voice said.

'A memory.'

'Yes. Tell me about that day.'

'It was when Ella was about eight months. It was the first time we all went to the beach as a family. Ella had bad colic, she cried and cried. It exhausted Anna. This was when things got better and we walked to a little quiet beach. Anna was lactating, she had these little pads to absorb her milk but she went through them in seconds. It left great wet pools on her bikini top, she was so embarrassed she kept going in the sea to hide it, we laughed for ages.'

'So why do you think she selected this picture, Richard?'

Tears built and then escaped down Richard's face. 'Because Anna wanted to say goodbye to the me when we were happy. For me to die remembered as I used to be I guess.'

'The memory is a powerful one?'

'Yes.'

'Richard, if I break this picture, if I smash the frame and tear up the photo, does the memory die?'

'No, of course not.'

'Why?'

'Why? That is a stupid question.'

'Indulge me, Richard.'

'Because, the memory isn't a thing, it's a, well, memories live inside you, live with you in your heart and your mind.'

'Memories are *permanent*, Richard, be they good or bad. Anything can recall them and they will be just as real as the time experienced. The best thing you ever did was make memories. But at some point during the course of your life you decided to make money instead. You have sewn salt to the soil of your family, so no good could grow, all is wasteland. You will need to start again and hope your family will suspend all memories of ill long enough for you to make good.'

'I don't know what you mean. You are talking in riddles.'

'Amnesia. A second chance. It isn't uncommon as a result of a coma. You don't have much time, Richard, you have not the luxury of time to rebuild what you have lost over years. But if they were to believe you don't remember anything, you will have an advantage, and you will need every advantage. Time is short.'

'What if I can't fix my mess?'

'I will still have to collect.'

'Okay.'

'You can move your fingers now, try.'

Richard needed the span of a heartbeat to think and for his fingers to respond. They slowly moved, followed by his toes. He smiled the most genuine smile his face had ever worn.

'I have to go, Richard, I cannot be here, a nurse will soon check you, and discover your recovery.'

'Wait, don't go.'

'Don't worry, I will help you, I won't be far.'

Richard was left to wait to be discovered, his body leaden and ravaged by pins and needles. He had sprouted cables and tubes, wires taped upon him. He felt like a potato when left and naked roots emerged from him like fingers to seek out soil. A long time he waited. Without his glasses, everything was slightly a blur, furry shapes busied past windows. A heavy weight of anxiety lay upon him and magnified the shortness of time to heal his family, yet he had no idea how to force the situation to meet his ends. *Amnesia? Does Gabriel really think I can fool a family to love me again in such a short time? That wasn't the task set though. It isn't their love I covet, it is for them to find love amongst themselves, and with the betterment of me not being around.*

The singing nurse was the one who discovered Richard awake. One of the few with the diligence to perform more than the minimum required of her job, she noticed his eyes open, following her about her tasks.

"Praise the lord!" she sang. "Praise the lord, and a good and long overdue morning to you, Mr Price." She quickly pressed the attention button and checked his vitals, busily seeking confirmation that he was indeed awake.

He was more than awake, Richard was being born again. Born into a lie and a life so short. He thought of himself as a butterfly, a brief life that carried such temporary purpose.

"Oh, Mr Price, it is so wonderful to see you. Can you understand me?" The words bounced out of the nurse like she was singing even when she talked. She moved the same, more dance than walk. Older than expected, tall and thin. Nothing like he had imagined. She looked remarkably like Morgan Freeman, the smell of biscuits drifted as she moved. He nodded a yes and set about trying to extract the serpentine tube that reached inside him. "Oh no you don't, Mr Price, I know you have waited a time but you must please be patient."

More nurses arrived, looking at each other aghast at his awakening. One retreated to find a doctor. He attempted to sit up but his arms only suggested the intention, gravity holding him firm to the mattress.

The nurse helped him sit. He pointed at the tubing.

"Okay, Mr Price, we will lose the endotrachea, but it will be very uncomfortable. My name is nurse Abby, tap on my hand if it hurts or you want me to pause."

The way she said Abby sounded like nurse *Happy*, and he liked her. The pipe dragged free, leaving its fleshy sleeve sore and dry. Richard coughed.

"Little sips," Abby said, passing him a small beaker of water that he took and eased to his crazy-paved lips.

* * *

When Anna arrived, it was much later in the day and Richard's elaborate deception was already long in play. To the world he had no idea who he was. He, however, worried as to how much he was supposed to recall in such cases. The doctors, who busied around, scheduled him for further tests and CT scans, but so far, Gabriel had been good on his word – other than muscle wastage and fake amnesia, with the exception of not actually knowing what happened to put him in his coma, he was fine. Anna, however, looked anything but. She looked horrified. Her mouth smiled, but her eyes said she was lying. She had lost weight, but not through worry, she was toned. Her hair returned to ebony from peppered with grey, and now cut short and modern. She glowed, and he hated that the only ruination of such beauty was her hiding her pain at seeing him in a growing state of repair. They shared a common guilt. He, for pushing the emotion on her, and her for taking it.

'Don't cry, you can't cry. Hide it, hide it for her.'

"I'm Richard," he said.

Anna looked about the room, at Richard and then to the staff, confused.

"This is your wife, Anna," Abby said. "He doesn't know who you are, he has amnesia."

"Is it permanent?" Anna enquired.

"Not usually. However, the brain never fully recovers."

"Fuck, you mean he is disabled? Mentally I mean?"

"No, he seems fine. But often the memories are never fully recovered, if at all. Personality changes have been known. It will be a difficult time for you both when he is home."

"Home? My home? You *are* kidding right?"

"Is that a problem? It is key for his recovery to be surrounded by people who love him."

"Good luck with *that*," Anna quipped.

"You will have help, he will have a full-time carer, so don't worry."

Richard watched the exchange, his wife feeling able to be as blunt and honest as she wished now her husband was a stranger, each word cold and lacerating his heart.

"Sorry, what was your name again?" he lied.

"ANNA!" she barked.

"Sorry," he looked and then picked at the woven blanket that covered his legs like a giant white knitted waffle.

"No, I'm sorry," she said. "You can't remember anything?"

He couldn't help it, the depth of her hatred so deep, the task seemingly futile, his bottom lip trembled. *Fight it, don't cry.* He couldn't dam the tears that began to rain, he tried to look away but had nowhere to hide.

"Oh God, I'm so sorry," Anna said. "You must be so frightened."

Richard nodded yes, because he was. Death knew of him and his grief advanced from a sense long ago lost. Ironically, his lies allowed him to at last be honest. "I'm horrible aren't I?"

Anna shifted from foot to foot uncomfortably and said nothing. Richard, however, hadn't needed her confirmation. He knew her hatred for him lay beyond a veil of temporary sympathy. He held the photo in the frame, and droplets fell onto baby Ella's glazed face. "You're beautiful, I must have been some kind of a catch to land a woman like you and some fool to turn you hate me." *Gabriel was wrong, Anna doesn't deserve this, she has suffered enough lies.* "I'm sure I can go somewhere else. I don't want to cause further pain."

Anna's hand fell over her mouth, involuntary, unexpected. Her eyes glossed wet and long-since-dead feelings minded. "You have to get better. The doctors know best, if that is what they suggest then that is what should happen. Do you remember anything?"

"No."

"Okay." She nodded.

"I don't even know what happened, how I got here," he said honestly.

"You had a stroke, Mr Price," Abby said. "You suffered a stroke due your lifestyle. Stress, diet et cetera. It produced a thrombus, a blood clot that travelled to your brain. We operated and the fatty deposit and blockage resolved. But you seemed to not recover and have been in a coma for eleven weeks."

Richard felt his head. The hair had remained cropped short post-surgery. His flowing, manicured locks gone. The reaction very real. By lifestyle he knew well they meant restaurants, whisky and cocaine.

"Are you sure it is alright for me to go *home*?"

"If it is what they say will be best," Anna replied.

Her love still existed for him, lost deep within the pages of the dark chronicles of their life, unseen and unread. He knew it. He felt it. He wished nothing more for her to love him again, yet knowing he would soon be gone, he chose not to chase her love only to abandon it once more. Anna had suffered enough.

* * *

Four days later, weakened and frail, they delivered him by ambulance to the house that ceased to be his home years past while both children were within. Once an old chapel school complete with spire, Richard had extended the building using local stone and on the south face, a glass annex now extended out onto a neighbouring field he had bought to accommodate it, like a symmetrical tumour. Where once would have been Victorian toilets stood vented barns that contained cars in carcoons. His prized collection that he lavished attention on as his surrogates for love, that now he had to pretend to have no knowledge of. Not that it mattered. He assumed they soon would be auctioned when he himself was turned to ash. The house itself a statement of arrogance. Finding something attractive that had stood for a century and deeming it inadequate, and then vandalise it with modern materials and surfaces was typical of him. The house was vulgar, but admitting so would have conceded that Anna was right.

Inside, however, was an entirely different affair. Anna's influence, organic and natural muted colours lifted wood and stone. Shelving made out of railway sleepers. And a carpet of linear multi-coloured lines that you would swear would be horrid, yet intelligently opened the hallway and trafficked to a remarkable island kitchen.

"Beautiful house," Richard said, "I live here?"

"Of sorts. You had – I mean *have* – a flat in London that you spend much time at." A salient reminder that the expectation was for him to be past tense.

"Is this my children's home too?" He asked what he already knew.

"They are not children any more. Ella, your daughter, is supposed to live here. Sam, your son, doesn't."

"Okay." Richard stood in the hall, upright only by the addition of a walking stick in each hand that trembled under strain from wasted limbs. He felt old, his steps preceded by cane and progress slow and sloth-like, as

Anna walked him to his room. Anna's kind heart always charitable, she had rebuilt her resolve since the shock of his recovery and agreed only to his temporary return for convalescence.

There had been no return from Gabriel, his guide, the not-an-angel – angel. Knowing now he had a surgery to his brain, his best guess was madness.

"This is you," Anna politely and pointlessly said as they both stood in a vast bedroom. "This was once your son's room, Samuel. You look like you need to rest. Your carer will be here soon and is sleeping in the room next door. So I will let you know when he gets here. He is nice, really helpful."

"Is he called Gabriel?"

"Gabriel? No, a foreign sounding name, I forget now. You should rest," she offered without a smile.

Richard sat on the edge of the bed, exhausted. He caught his breath and considered the mess he was in. He fell back to lie on the bed and listened to the distant clatter of Anna in the kitchen. She was once an awful cook and a subject of joyous ridicule. When first together it was still a time when women were not so much condemned but more suggested to be home-makers. They didn't have much and Anna didn't want much, just a family and a dog. He, however, became poisoned with loftier ambitions. There was some erroneous belief that women magically knew how to cook, as if by some celestial instinct. Anna would create some horrendous meals that they both ate with laughter. Once she bought a pie in a tin and placed it in the oven without removing the lid. The resulting explosion took the door off. For the next half year he worked overtime to replace the oven and until he could, their meals consisted of solely stove-top dishes while the oven became a bread bin in their space-limited flat. Anna was now a wonderful cook, creative and informed. The field that once lay to waste to allow his horrid glass structure now a giant allotment that she farmed for seasonal produce.

The warmth of the memory was woefully short, knowing she would have been happy to have stayed in a tiny flat if he lost everything. He had come close on more than one occasion. He would suffer at the hands of pride and ego to return to such squalor as he saw it. Anna, however, would have been fine.

He decided it best to leave Anna to her life, to leave. Even tell her he had a visit from an imaginary angel and might be clinically insane, yet too much muscle lay dormant and he couldn't sit up to get off the bed. He could roll, though. He rolled so he could slip from the bed onto the floor, landing ungainly on his hands and knees. Richard needed to pull himself up from the bed, but the bed was pushed close to the wardrobe and he hadn't the space to turn, having no choice but to back out like a reversing human car. As he retreated, a drumming applause accompanied him. Richard turned as best he could to see a large white boxer dog wobbling with excitement at seeing him, its tail hitting the wall then the door in a steady rhythm.

"Go away, dog."

The dog jumped at the vocal incitement to play, lowering itself on its haunches to wobble more vigorously and tail drumming faster. The dog seemed friendly enough, so he continued to back-up rear first.

"Go on! Go away dog."

The dog bounced and wagged with such joy its head now wagged too. It was all too much and had to join in the fun. As Richard retreated the big dog mounted him from behind, thrusting its hips sexually.

"Oi!" He couldn't help but laugh. Embarrassed but

knowing he would have to call for help, his attempt to cry for freedom ended when another little golden hairy dog appeared between his arms and started licking his face with fury. Needing both arms to remain upright, he couldn't defend from the little dog painting his face and mouth with its wet tongue. Richard found himself hostage to both the dogs.

"Oh Christ!" Anna said, before calling her dog, "MOJO! Get off him."

"Here, let me help you," a warm male voice said as two sinewy arms enveloped him, helping him upright. The man was foreign-looking with tanned skin, mahogany eyes set in thick long black lashes, the features delicate yet sat above a square, manly jaw and topped with a mane of black obsidian hair. Perfect teeth beamed.

"Richard, this is your carer, he's the guy who is going to help you get better," Anna said.

"Nice to see you are making friends," the man said.

Richard was pleased he was his carer as initially he thought it might have been Brian, Anna's lover. Once upright, Richard found himself taller than the man, who stood about five-foot-six. He wore a necklace of ethnic beads on a leather lace, a faded and baggy t-shirt with a graffiti 'Who?' logo on it with tatty worn jeans. Disappointment lingered that he wasn't Gabriel.

"Yama," he said, extending a hand that Richard shook. "Well, the dogs like you," Yama laughed.

Anna excused herself, and escorted the dogs out of the room. Richard returned to sitting on the edge of the bed, his hands firmly pressed between his knees. Yama pulled up a chair and sat.

"You look disappointed, Richard. Is there something wrong?"

"Aside from the obvious?" he tried to joke. "I was

expecting someone else, that's all. I'm fine."

"Gabriel?"

"Yes, Gabriel."

"I told you I have many names, Michael, Gabriel, here, and for as long as I am to help you, I am Yama."

"Oh, thank God, I thought I was going crazy, that you were a figment of madness. Why Yama?"

"Because I like it and it's not Gabriel."

"What is wrong with Gabriel?"

"Nothing is wrong with Gabriel, other than you chose Gabriel, not I. You didn't ask which one I prefer, you chose and you have to learn you don't always get what you want…"

"I hardly always get what I want. Look at my situation now."

"The only way you will find an end is to be honest. However, your situation is so dire that you have to start on a foundation of a lie. What does that tell you?"

"I know," Richard nodded.

"No, you don't. You tried so hard to make your son something other than he is. But guess what, he *is* what he *is*. And you, for all your bullying, could not change that. Your daughter the same. You wanted her to be different, wanting her to exploit the fruits that fell from your tree."

"I never tried to change Anna," Richard offered as a defence.

"No. Instead you let her fall in love with a man that you thought wasn't good enough – you. So you chased that pot of gold at the end of the rainbow and bought her loyalty with things. You tried so hard to become the man you thought she should love that you became the very man she didn't."

"That is hardly fair. We have been together thirty years, nobody stays the same. We all change, life changes us."

"Has Anna changed?"

Richard inspected his white alabaster skin that seemed to have death already within it. "No."

"For all your bullying, have your children changed?"

"Not for the better."

"All you have done is convince them to not love you, rather than convince them to be clones of you."

He watched tears fall to his death-white hand and chase away over the valleys of his skin, clinging to his finger before falling. The droplet appeared to be rushing as if it too hated him.

"You need to live in the moment, Richard. You don't know how long you have left. It is important you under-stand, *live in the moment.*" Yama stressed the words. "Get some rest. You need your strength."

* * *

Some hours later, Richard woke to silence. At his third attempt he was able to sit up. Again aided by canes, he moved slowly and how he imagined Salvador Dali elephants would walk, lumbering and ungainly. He called to the empty house. In the kitchen the fridge hummed and a large clock ticked. The surfaces were impeccably clean and smelt of lemon, suggesting a recent tidy and that Anna wasn't far. In the front room, the little golden dog was curled on the sofa that had messy blankets and a liberal coating of dog hair. The house seemed vacant. It was a distant barking that drew his attention outside.

In the field were Anna and Yama, the white boxer barking and orbiting them both in a 'play with me' run.

Progress outside was slow. The dog saw him first, and missiled toward him then stopped, wagging his tail with such gusto that he bent double. A paw streaked brown soil down his trouser leg before the dog retreated back to Anna, who on seeing him finished whatever was she was doing. They both strolled leisurely back to the house. Their faces ruddy and red from the chill of an unseasonally cold May, both beaming from the laughter they had both enjoyed, and that tortured Richard with envy.

"How are you feeling?" Anna asked.

"Better," he said, abruptly.

"How is your memory?" she asked again.

"Same."

"Look." Yama held up a wicker basket full of leafy green and finger-like storks, "Fresh asparagus and kale, how amazing is that?"

"Wonderful," he said sarcastically.

Anna's happy glow was stolen, replaced with one of contempt. Richard hated his theft of her joy. "I will make some coffee," she said. "I bet you are a coffee man, Yama?"

"Hells yeah," he chirped. Then turned to Richard as Anna retired inside. "So, still treating people like possessions I see?"

"You were flirting with my wife, I saw you."

"So?"

"You're a fucking angel? I mean, what the hell?"

"You lot think it was me as Gabriel that got Mary pregnant, remember?"

"What?"

"Baby Jesus, it's in a book," Yama mocked. "Walk with me Richard."

"No," Richard said, searching for a cigarette but having none.

"You will."

Eventually Richard did.

They walked slowly over the lawns, over a gravel drive and headed to the barn of cars. Yama released the clasps and slid the door, revealing the tents with cars within, like gestating prizes inside wombs of wealth.

"You realise you will have to lie on top of another lie now."

"What do you mean?"

"To Anna, you can't be jealous as you are supposed to not remember anything. And so you will have to lie, *again*, and invent some excuse. Did you see how easy it was to feel affronted that things are not as you want?"

Richard remained silent, guilt needing no expression.

"Tell me about the cars, Richard."

"These are my babies. The one thing I did right, and a very highly regarded collection. This," Richard pointed to the first tent, "in here is a genuine and un-restored 73 Porsche Carrera RS, just beautiful and with less than 18k on the clock." Walking to the next, "Here is, what I think one of the most beautiful cars ever made, a 68 Dino, it isn't supposed to be a Ferrari but, it is. I do have another special Ferrari though, over to the back is a Daytona. The 365 GTB four. Stunning metal."

"The cars have to go."

"What? That isn't going to happen."

"Richard, it is."

"No. It isn't."

"If you don't sell them, when you die, Anna will. They are just cars. They will, at some point, be sold on."

"I love those cars."

"No Richard, you don't. You love owning them, you love possessing them. You love the boastful currency they give in having them and the reaction of envy from peers. If you loved them you would have used them, enjoyed them. They are compliant and inanimate. Unlike family, they will sit in these *things* forever without protest. Held in stasis until one day you might let the sun to shine upon them.

This is how you treat your family, Richard."

"That's not true."

"Isn't it? I was just laughing with Anna and you were jealous."

"Because I still love her, Yama, it is simply that."

"If that were true, you would have spent more time here, yet you spent as much time as possible in London. You had relations with other women that you had the audacity to allow to continue with a growing lack of discretion. How exactly is it different? If you were honest, you expected Anna to be here, unchanged, like the cars. You didn't like me talking to her because you view her as yours, a possession. Let me ask you, Richard, when was the last time you used any of these cars?"

Richard shook his head. Time told lies just as he did. The reality was, though it felt recent it was beyond years. "They are appreciating assets though. Lack of use isn't a bad thing."

"That might well be the case with cars, but it is hardly the case with people, Richard."

He nodded at the painful metaphor, knowing any one of these cars would be loved by an enthusiast rather than a collector.

"You don't own anything. Nobody does, everything is temporary on a greater time line. Tell me, Richard, if you could keep just one, which would it be?"

He thought long and hard about the differing cars, basing his decision on looks, then value, then performance. Then, if time allowed, which one he could use with his family. It had to have four seats. This edited his choice down to only two cars, the Daytona and a long-wheelbase Mercedes Pagoda. In the end he pipped for the Daytona.

"Both Sam and Ella are coming over tomorrow and we are going to play a game. We will ask them to choose a car too, let's see which car they would pick."

* * *

In the kitchen, Anna was working on a recipe, finding a creative use for the asparagus. Richard and Yama returned, and sat upon the heavy wooden chairs that circled the table.

Richard took a deep breath, then sighed. "Anna, I'm sorry."

"What for?" she said, looking up, but not at him. Gentle neck, soft features.

"For being rude earlier, abrupt. I get frustrated and I'm sorry."

"That's okay. It's understandable."

Anna, still forgiving after all this time. She always looked for the best in people. "And, I'm sorry for everything else."

"Pardon?" Anna put down her glasses confused by the apology.

"I am sorry. For how I used to treat you, for, everything. All of it. I can tell it was my fault. And I am sorry."

Anna felt moved by the gesture. However, believing the Richard in her kitchen was temporary, she enjoyed it but didn't feel the comment. Instead she chose to defer its consideration and pour each of them a coffee.

Richard watched the steam swirl and reach skyward. "Your kitchen is wonderful."

"It's okay," Anna remarked, "not how I would have it."

This shocked Richard, he thought this was her love, her dream. "How would you have it?"

"Well, I often asked Richard, sorry, you, if I could have a wood-burning stove, that heated water and ovens. Something less fancy and more ecological. He ignored me.

You ignored me. Saying it would devalue the kitchen."

"So, change it. We have the money don't we?" he asked, wanting her to have her will.

Anna laughed and clapped, "Can I keep him?" she joked with Yama. "I like this version of him. You do, *you* have the money, Richard."

"Then change it. Get a wood-burner fitted. What is the point of money if it isn't used. I will go to the bank."

"Richard," Yama said, "you have been in a coma for months, your accounts are locked down. You can't just walk in, they will not think of you having sound mind."

"Then sell the cars." The realisation of what true value meant was now blinding. "It's not like I use them. Sell them."

"You will think differently when you get your memory back." Anna slid her chair back that seemed to protest for her as it dragged along the slate floor. "It's just an oven."

"No, I don't think I will. Because I might remember things doesn't mean I will feel or think any differently as I do now. Besides, value should be based on what enjoyment you get from the kitchen, not what it is worth. I'm guessing you spend hours in here, weeks even, and every time you think about how much you wish it was how *you* wanted it, not me."

"Are you serious?" Her face glowed. He wanted to reach out and touch her, warn her he was leaving, tell her he never stopped loving her.

"Yes, I am serious. It is pointless having cars I don't use with great value, and denying you something you would use every day and get much enjoyment from."

Anna sat forward. She placed her mug on the table and looked at Richard for a time. Something stirred. Within the lost and chased-away love, overgrown with the tendrils and roots of disappointment and neglect, hope fluttered.

"Richard, is that you?" she mocked.

"Are Samuel and Ella still visiting tomorrow?" Yama asked.

"Ella isn't going on holiday now, so she is. Sam didn't say yes. But I hope he will."

"Did you ask them both to bring something that is a keepsake?"

"Yes," Anna replied. "However, both Ella's and mine are here. Sam said he wouldn't though, so..." She looked painfully at the floor.

Anna prepared lunch and talked. Richard listened. For once he didn't just hear; he listened to every word, its hope and its meaning, how every letter sounded escaping from her soft lips. Much of the conversation centred on the garden. He asked questions just to hear her speak without the venom and bile that was the norm when both were this close. She spoke of such passion, of the dreams for the square of earth. Grapes for wine and a butterfly garden. She took not one thing for granted. Richard felt ever more humbled, numb, as if the coma crept up on him many years ago. Whenever she stopped, he would ask another question just to hear her talk again, carefully avoiding issues that demanded discussion, choosing to defer the storm of confrontation.

Anna's head listed to one side in a sudden recognition, and she smiled.

"What is it?" he asked.

"We used to talk like this all the time. Remember?" Then, realising what she said, "Of course you don't, sorry. We lived in places without gardens. We used to drive into the country to escape the masses and find a field to just lie there. I would talk and talk, and I was sure you had switched off, as if I had become background noise. You'd say, 'Go on, you were saying,' just to let me know you were listening."

He remembered perfectly and suffered a painful longing for those halcyon days. The accidental reconciliation brought about an awkwardness to the proceedings. Sensing an ending, Richard excused himself using the guise of needing to rest.

Yama helped Richard to his room. He feared the confrontation due the following day. The ensuing days would be spent dredging the wastes and relics of the mess lain in his wake, consequences and collaterals, a hurried search for reconciliation. He felt exhausted. Ella might be easy to glue back in place, her waywardness one of reaction to the boreal cold that occupied the space left by an absent father. Samuel, however, was a loss he thought about and that hurt every day. Sam was his weakness to hold onto what his pride had chased away.

Fatigue brought sleep. Anna and Yama laughing returned him awake. He listened to them talking, her laughter boiled his blood but he knew he had to let it be, and so allow it to cool. He had to be comfortable to lose what wasn't his. Each time laughter punched him awake, he would look at his watch at the hours passing.

Ella's voice announced her early arrival the following day, and she excited the already excited greeting of the dogs. The boxer's tail drummed off a radiator and sounded like a steel band, the little dog yapped a piercing volume. Richard celebrated her arrival with his stomach doing flip-flops. His little girl, his angel, who only days past cared little about his pending demise. Richard tried to make Sam strong, unknowing that he was already armour-plated. Ella, however, was his little girl. Her face would make him smile, no matter what she had done or the unspeakable depth of bad mood he was in. Blame often placed at her brother's feet instead of hers. The excuse being he was older, should set an example. Anything to defer from shouting at his girl. Ella was a mirror that reflected the worst in him, believed his lies. She blamed her mother for his rampant nonattendance. The battles grew shorter, the absence longer. After each hostile engagement, he would foster allies, his only being a little girl, who, when hearing *'Mummy doesn't understand'* and *'I am doing all this for you, because you like nice things too'*, believed him. He knew then that he taught his little girl to value material things over family. A lesson he knew to be wrong, but he cowardly needed a supporter of his cause. A lesson he thought would unravel by itself over time but didn't.

Ella enjoyed preferential treatment and blamed her mother for Daddy not being around, right up to when she woke one morning to find Mummy crying, and the lies collapsed, leaving a painful disengaged and distant relationship between her and her mother, and a newly found hatred for her father. She slipped between the two factions and medicated away her pain with substances.

Richard found himself able to walk on one cane, maybe because he wanted to seem less vulnerable to his daughter. Yama stuck his head around the door to inform him that Ella was there and to come to the kitchen. It took a while to get there, the smell of patchouli oil reached him first. *Ella must be the last person on the planet to use patchouli to do what it is supposed, mask cannabis.* Once in the kitchen, Ella looked like she had come straight from a club, or at best slept for an hour after a club. Her make-up heavy, hair wild and dress short. Anna stood leaning against the side, glaring at her.

"What? I've jeans and a top in my bag."

They were both doing their best to be amicable and score points at the same time. An awkwardness of trying to avoid a fight as naturally early as they usually happened was sadly evident.

"Oh look, it's Daddy," she said sarcastically.

"Hostility is not going to help," Yama intervened early.

"Who are you again?" she barked.

Yama smiled, his face tanned and kind, strong and handsome. Ella tried to look away and Yama shifted to maintain eye contact using a big beaming smile that would disarm the most fierce soul. "Yama, I'm your dad's carer."

Ella tried to look away but couldn't, her anger one of habit rather than reason, and a smile appeared slowly.

"Yama? What kind of fucking name is that?"

"I'm from Iraq. My name is Yama Azrael."

"Iraq? Fuck." Ella looked shocked.

"Don't worry I didn't bring my bomb with me today." The room filled with a muted laughter.

"I didn't mean it like that, I'd have said you were Greek or Turkish, not an Arab. Ugh, *assalamu*." She smiled attempting her best Arabic hello.

"Oh," Yama sat up and laughed. "I'm impressed, where did you learn that?"

"Saudi, I holiday there often."

"You know, Turks are Arabs, well most. Some are Kurdish like me, I am not an Arab. So hello in Kurdish, my language would be, as I consider us friends, *Rozh bash*." Yama held out his hand and held and shook Ella's.

Ella beamed. "*Rozh bash*," she replied.

"There, that's one more radicalised," Yama joked. Laughter chased away the atmosphere.

"So, how are you, Dad?"

"Getting better."

"Do you remember anything yet?"

"Nothing. Except for what has taken place since waking up."

"That must be hard? Will you get your memory back?"

"I don't know," he lied.

"Is Sam here yet?"

"No. Not yet," Anna replied.

"Is he coming?" Ella asked.

"He said he is, but who knows."

The conversation continued, natural organic conversation, with both his wife and daughter engaged and not fighting. Ella gave the version of herself she wanted her father to believe and with his ever-dissolving time left, he listened, his newfound skill. Ella was a woman and he treated her like a child. Ella lied about what she was doing with her life, equine studies suspended for clubbing and the exuberance that its culture provided. She partied and had no direction in life, but what she did have was time. *She is young, let her be young,* Richard conceded. Ella asked to excuse herself and to grab a shower.

"Before you do, there is something we need you to do," Yama asked. "Could you look about the barn? Your dad is going to sell the cars. All but one, have a look and select the one you'd want to keep."

"For him or for me?" Ella asked.

"Doesn't matter. Your choice."

"Okay," she said, removing a pouch of rolling tobacco and lighter. "Is this a game, or is he really selling the cars? Because he would never sell those cars." The words a statement rather than question. The dogs accompanied her to the barn.

Richard wanted to be as close as he could to Anna, and so joined her as they walked to the garden so she could dig up supper.

"You need to choose a car too," Richard said.

"What is this about?"

"I'm not sure, it is Yama's idea. But you should keep one anyway."

"I already know which one I would keep."

"Really?" Richard was surprised at the comment, she had never showed any interest in the collection before. "Well don't tell me yet, let's do as Yama suggests."

The sun was getting high as midday approached. A veil of mist hovered a foot above the ground like the field lay wrapped in a silk scarf as Anna set about her toil. Richard stood and witnessed how busy the wildlife was. Bees slowly landed poorly from flower to flower, appearing to fail to cling on only to fly to the next and do the same. This was at odds with the hyperactive wild flapping of butterflies that seemed to have no sense of direction yet somehow managed to banquet on Anna's efforts. Gnats held a holding pattern like miniature planes waiting to land, and small birds in little squadrons landed on the wire divisions Anna laid, looking lost. The field was a mess, Anna doing it her way. If he had intervened there would have been straight lines, structure and separation. The field would have been a vista of pointless regulation and order that offered no further harvest. Anna enjoyed the chaos. Sticks of bamboo supported vines, patches of naked soil aside what best could be described as clumps of purple or green or expanses under messy plastic. There was a freedom to the sprawl that he wished he could learn. Adopt the *what will be, will be* attitude. Richard did learn, however, that contrary to his previous beliefs, hindsight without question offered some of the best teachings.

Much later in the day, the hole in the corroded exhaust on Sam's tatty old Renault told of his late arrival and that confrontation had arrived with him. Considering what little time he might have left, Richard shut his eyes and smiled at the sun, enjoying its warm embrace. Anna worked the earth, backlit by the sun so she wore a golden halo, that made gnats glow as if she was orbited by stars.

He was such a fool to squander the love of someone who'd have loved him regardless of how little he had.

After some time enjoying the little time he had left, Richard drew a deep breath and expelled it with a burdened sigh. Sam – he couldn't put it off any longer. A feud that was every bit his fault, and that hurt every day.

Sam had inherited his stubbornness and so reconciliation became the victim of time and pride. He turned to return to the house, up ahead Sam and Yama, deep in discussion, were walking off to the distant woodland, Sam's camera bags in hand.

It was late afternoon when they returned. Richard had been enjoying the calm reprieve his lie provided, allowing Anna and Ella to share space without throwing accusation or insult. Yama's infectious laugh was heard from outside along with the clunking of car doors closing. He worried Sam was just leaving and didn't care enough to stay, nerves of how to manage what happened next were welcome as they both entered the house.

"Well, that's just it," Sam said. "The anti-digital stuff is fucking bullshit. Without doubt, Ansel Adams would have embraced digital, without doubt."

"I agree. But, I still love those who still use stuff like plate cameras, y'know, like Joe Cornish," Yama chimed.

"Love Joe Cornish's stuff. But you know that is a digital back on a plate camera right? Still digital photography." Sam placed his now-muddy shoes in the hall, and stood in mustard chunky-knit socks. Richard had the good fortune of him being mostly disarmed by Yama, but just looking at his father he stiffened. Defined high cheekbones and a perfectly straight nose, much of his looks came from his mother, his hair cropped short allowing his handsomeness to sing. Sam had his mother's artistic flair too that showed in his impeccable style and talent as a photographer. Yet he was burdened with his father's stubbornness and resolve.

"Come on," Yama said, "did you bring an item to use like asked?"

"There is nothing that exists in this world that has any fond memories of him."

"You have your choice of car though, yes?"

"Yeah," Sam grumbled, "I've made a choice. But, before we get started, I want it clear that I want to rebuild a relationship with Mum and Ella, I don't want that fucking man in my life."

"Sam," Yama said. "Nothing is permanent, nothing stays the same, you have every right to say such, but also every choice. Things can be different, though what you do is up to you."

Sam positioned himself on the furthest chair from his father, choosing tea over coffee.

Anna stood, the emotion of the refugees of her family in ruin around a table that was once their home. Feelings compressed, naked and exposed. "Sam, it is lovely to see you. I've missed you. So much." Her words were wet, her eyes equally so, pooled with tears, as were Sam's.

By the time Sam stood, Anna had already closed the space between them and pulled him close. Ella enveloped them both and they remained entwined, knotted together. If he could fossilise that moment and ensure no further detachment, he would be happy to go. Richard for the first time considered when. Did he get a choice? Could he decide the date? Either way, if his passing now ensured his family's union, he would offer himself willingly. Richard sat on the fringe, the pariah, left to witness his damage trying to repair itself.

After a moment to grieve that became an age, Yama lead them all into the living room. One of the chairs had been moved so it sat directly opposite the sofa that was

Richard's place.

"So," Yama said, "this is to help stir memories for Richard, but it is clear, this family has some healing to do too. So – heal." Yama laughed. "Starting with the car you chose, who wants to go first?" The room returned detached, nobody ventured. "Okay, I will pick – Ella, your car and why?"

"The red one covered in dust under the tarpaulin and cardboard, the old one."

"She means the MGB, the convertible," Sam helped.

"And why?"

"Because we had fun in that car. I loved Dad driving us to school in it and screaming at the leaks in the roof. We used to try to block them with our fingers. On sunny days, driving to the beach, me and Sam in the tiny back seat, singing our hearts out and when it was safe, like along the massive car park in front of the beach we went to, we would sit on the back of the car with our feet on its seat like we were flying. Good times." Ella's joyous remembrance drifted into a pained longing.

Richard listened. Each word a truth that gently landed like a snowflake, yet burned with guilt.

"And your item?"

Ella produced a small stuffed elephant – pink, with skin made of towelling. Time and use hadn't been kind to it, it appeared misshaped and worn. "This is Ellynoonooh," she said. "I loved Nooh, I used to rub its trunk on my nose and when sleepy, stuff the trunk up my nose. It was gross, the trunk got matted and thick with snot. Mum and Dad would sneak it off me and wash it in the night and put it back by morning."

"Is that why you had picked it?" Yama asked.

"No..." Ella started to speak, but then emotion stole her words. Remembering meant revisiting a love that was so pure and true, but also acknowledging its passing. Ella apologised as tears fell and breathing became brittle. "I chose Ellynoonooh because of one time we were in town. We used to go into the city to a café when Mum and Dad could afford it. Back then money was harder to find. On our walk from the café to the car I dropped Nooh. I must have been three, maybe four? But I was distraught. I cried and cried. Dad went to look for it and came back empty. He told Mum to take us home. Daddy stayed out all night searching, walked to the depot of the bin collectors to search their unit before it all got delivered to the dump. I cried myself to sleep, but in the morning Ellynoonooh was back and washed. Daddy searched all night. Daddy used to make everything better back then." Ella fell ruined by grief. Anna held her and Richard could almost hear the lost souls finding each other and bonding back in place.

Don't cry. You can't let them know you remember.

"Anna, when you're ready, it's your turn. Which car?"

"Same car, the MGB. It was the first car Richard got that wasn't a 'shitter' as he called them. He took me to hospital to give birth to both Samuel and Ella in it. We had good times in that car. I can name hundreds of them, camping, beaches, pushing it when we couldn't work out how the battery kept draining. There is even pen over the back seat where Sam drew something and Rich went crazy. Even though it reminds me of the start of the bad times in some ways, if I had to choose, it would be that."

"If you don't mind, can you say more about the bad times, as it might help trigger emotions and kick-start recollection." As Anna spoke, Yama watched Richard, who in turn felt his scrutiny as every word cut deeply.

"Oh. Well, the MGB started his love for cars. He bought and sold cars and then started working in dealerships. He changed back then I think. The people he worked with were arrogant and womanisers, real assholes. Richard hated them at first but we needed the money. He would say how wrong it was, people would come in for a car and be sold something out of their budget, finance, insurance and such. But he got addicted to the money and started viewing both cars and people as, I don't know, commodities, assets. When he started his own dealerships it was bad. We argued all the time. Then cars were no longer enough. He bought the land then more land and it became commercial property. It wasn't about cars any more, just money. It was all he cared about." Unlike Ella, the memory brought Anna anger.

"And your item?"

Anna held up a Wham CD, 'Club Tropicana' the cover faded, the plastic case scratched from the many years so it appeared diffused. "Wham," she said laughing, "this was when CD players first came out and the car dealership bought two by mistake so Rich pinched one. The only CD we could afford was Wham. We played it over and over," Anna clapped with laughter. "Rich hated Wham, but it was like brainwashing. I can't remember what the fight was about now, but when I came home, Rich organised a Wham party for just the two of us just to cheer me up. It was hilarious. There was a fizzy drink back then called 'Tropicana' that we drank in mugs laced with vodka, dressed like we were at the beach and just danced to Wham all night. I don't think I've ever laughed as much since. We had such fun times. Once."

Anna didn't cry. Her tears for him long gone, but each reminiscence raked the shallows of him, lifting memories like fallen leaves from the mire where they lay. His actions and lack of, his sole warrant for change.

"Thank you, Anna," Yama said, turning to Sam. It was clear the sharing had advanced his venom further to the surface rather than appeased it. "Sam, are you ready?"

"I will try," he said, but shook his head gently, suggesting he couldn't.

"The car, let's start at an easy place. What is your choice?"

"Same. The red MGB, same reasons, I guess."

"Can you share? Elaborate more?"

Sam stood, brushed his thighs free from dog hair and looked at his father, defiant. He sought no restoration of what once existed. The remnants of what lay broken were the results of a deeper pain, the abandonment more severe.

"You know what? He can go fuck himself. I want no part of this."

Anna stood, and offered an anaemic challenge, "Sam, he is still your father."

"He is nothing to me, and I want no part in his recovery. I would rather him suffer."

"Sam!" Anna protested with more vigour.

"Don't you fucking dare," he snarled, "You have no right, you stood by that fucking bully, I'd be happy if I never saw him again. This was a mistake. I'm going."

Anna stood but it was Ella who tried to hold him in place, begging him to stay, but he wouldn't be held. He apologised to his sister, blamed his mother and left. The pain so great Richard had to hold on to his chair for fear of falling. Just as his family seemed to heal, everything unfurled to the mess that existed before, the undoing hit like a squalling storm. Sam left, making it clear he had no intention to ever return.

"Maybe we are lucky that we can't remember, maybe you shouldn't bother getting your memory back," Ella said, wiping her nose on her sleeve and failing to roll a cigarette with her now-trembling hands.

"What do you mean *we*?" Richard asked.

"Us, me and you. I can hardly remember a thing. I remember all the fighting, I remember you and Mum screaming night after night. I remember so many times your things in bin liners for you to collect and then you both used to pretend nothing happened afterwards. The following morning, when Dad was gone, you made out all was okay. You acted happier. Even when Dad came home you both acted like we imagined it. You would fight and pretend, fight and pretend. I remember sneaking into Samuel's room and us crying together. But everything else is gone. Your fighting did that. It bleached all my memories, everything is gone. I can't remember birthdays I had, friends at school, holidays, events, nothing. It is as if all I remember is fighting and just empty space. The thing Yama asked us to do, bring an item to remember works because once I see something I can remember, but without a prompt it's all gone."

It was then that Anna broke, not from the afflictions Richard had caused, she had thick tough scars against such traumas, but from the trauma of her girl, the fallout clear from their ritual battles. "I'm so sorry, Ella. Richard, maybe this isn't such a good idea."

"It's not just him. It is you too," Ella said. "Whisky, the smell makes me sick. One whiff and I see the glasses of it you hid about the house, and the stink of it in mugs when you hid it in coffee. Fruit juice too, because that was put in vodka and you said it was juice when you lied about getting better. I remember not getting picked up from school a lot but not the school."

"Did you ever tell me you were drinking?" Richard asked, knowing she didn't.

"You were never around to tell. You were worse, at least I was home and it was *just* drinking."

"I'm sorry," Richard said again. He felt like the cold

wind that caused tornados, that when close enough to his family, the forces would clash into a spinning column of pain. Anna embraced her daughter, she not without blame but her misgivings a symptom of her own abandonment.

Richard returned to his room accompanied by Yama. His wife and daughter had much to share.

"I don't think I can do this," Richard said.

"Why, because it is painful?"

"Yes."

"You asked me to help, I am helping. Did you think I was going to put my hand into a pouch and throw pixie dust over them and declare *'Ta-daa, all is fixed!'*? It hurts because life is painful, the consequences of your actions are painful. Are you going to lie to me too and tell me you didn't know the hurt you were causing?"

"I didn't think about it."

"Yes, you did. You learned not to acknowledge it though. Much like you learned to not mind you were making people buy what they couldn't afford. Do you remember how you felt the first time you had to coerce a family into long finance agreements to buy a car they couldn't afford? Remember how it turned your stomach? Do you recall the change to applauding yourself and those who worked for you when they did the same? The reward from such selfishness is fruit that falls from a poisoned tree. No good comes of it. You did the things you did because they were fun, because family was work, you knew full well of their suffering and chose not to care. You substituted yourself with money."

"Why are you doing this? I can't change the past!"

"Remember the picture, Richard. If I destroyed it, the memories remain? Well, the same happens when you try to bury the memories or drown them in whisky. There is always a victim to your actions and their memories are permanent too. Knowing isn't understanding. Apologising isn't owning. When death comes, your family's union is dependent on the alignment of truth. Each of the breakages in your family need to line up to heal, or it will remain broken."

Richard sobbed, grieving for the time lost, and the effects of such puerile endeavours on those who offered love unconditional.

"My Samuel, I need to make it right, explain."

"Yes. You do."

"Tomorrow, I will go talk to him, see if I can make him see sense."

"There you go again, Richard, Samuel sees sense perfectly, are you suggesting his recollections are wrong or that he should only see things as you wish him to?"

"I mean, ask him to forgive and to know his family need him."

"You need to rest. I have to spend time with Anna and Ella. You have a physically demanding day tomorrow."

Richard sat up, concerned. "I'm only just walking on one cane."

"Tomorrow we rehabilitate body and mind. It will be fun. You golf right?"

"Yes," Richard lifted upon the glimmer of Joy. "I love golf."

* * *

Richard watched Anna and Ella holding hands as they walked to the field. His daughter seemed like a little girl again. Fire stretched across the sky as the sun battled with the onset of night, its warmth giving rise to late activity: to starlings that swooped and dipped in a cloud of birds that would split and rejoin, lifting and tumbling. A joy to witness and a spectacle performed to a chorus of song from other birds already hunkered inside the trees that whispered in the late evening trade winds.

Richard sat on the step outside the kitchen and watched Yama wander in long baggy shorts and tattered flip-flops across the field to join his wife and daughter. It wasn't long before laughter returned, such was the affection of Yama. Even the sun seemed to linger longer to hang on to his every word. *What is he?* Richard wondered. *If not an angel then what? Is he an angel in everything but title? Sent here to save us, and if so why when we had such good fortune squandered?* Richard postponed such deep considerations for a later date and decided to simply enjoy what time he had left watching Anna and Ella laughing, the purest pleasure a husband and father could ever attest.

"Dad," Ella shook Richard awake. His eyes blinked in the gloom but smiled at seeing his daughter's pretty face. "C'mon, Daddy, it's time to go. Yama is waiting."

"What?" He rubbed stone from his eyes. He didn't want to go, he wanted to look at his child's face. "Where?"

"The beach."

"What? What time is it?"

"Five, let's go."

"In the morning?"

"Yes, in the morning, let's go."

Richard stood in the hall, his hair reflecting the mess he felt inside. Ella looked glowing with excitement, and that alone he couldn't disappoint.

"Ready?"

"Yes, but what for?"

"You will see," Yama said, taking Richard by the arm and dragging him to outside where he opened the back doors of a tatty van. "Throw your wetsuit in there," he said to Ella who complied, throwing a light blue neoprene suit inside.

"Wetsuit?" Richard asked still asleep.

"Yes. Wetsuit."

"Why?"

"Surfing."

Inside the cabin of the van, the seats were three abreast, a scented necklace of flowers hung from the mirror along with a worn, faded and now scentless cardboard wave on elastic. Yama climbed behind the wheel, Ella beside him in the middle and Richard reservedly climbed in and sat on the last free seat. The dashboard upholstered with a satin of dust and the remains of a block of surfboard wax melted in the corner of the window. He again questioned his sanity, *Angels are not supposed to transport themselves in tatty vans.*

'I'm not an angel.' A voice popped into his head like a thought of his own.

"Surfing? Aren't I a little old for surfing?"

"You are fifty-three, Richard, the world champion of surfing is forty. Kelly will probably be champion when he is your age too."

"Why so early?"

"It's a lesson. Trust me," Yama said, accompanied by Ella's laughter, something he thought he might never hear again. How could he protest?

"Ben Howard," Yama continued, "sing us to the beach," reaching to select music to play from a scuffed iPod touch that hung from a musical umbilical cord connecting it to an even tattier stereo.

Empty roads became empty lanes, as if they had discovered the planet abandoned, the sky pink with the sun's return. Hedgerows became more unruly as the houses thinned to rural fields and to native gorse and fauna. The road itself became a patchwork of old blacktop with spotted repairs and potholes, descending from the crest of a valley becoming a rough muddy track that coiled and snaked, showing the tracks of tractors. The lane opened out to a sandy bank knitted together by reed and grass that gently sloped to beach. Golden sand turned brown where it met the sea. Foaming broken waves washed up the beach, overturning shells and pebbles as they retreated, the sand undisturbed. Grey undulating lines would approach the shoreline in sets, build into waves and break, bright white water chasing along walls of water until close enough to collapse in the shallows.

"It is so beautiful here," Ella said, looking out to the ocean.

Yama opened the back of his van and threw Ella her wetsuit, followed by another at Richard. "Might be a bit long, but it will fit you."

"I haven't any trunks." Richard started to make his excuses.

"So, wear pants, or nothing, it's up to you." From within, Yama withdrew a long glossy board, white with two equal long thick red stripes, the deck mottled lumpy white where wax had been applied, and dirtied from sand and wetsuit. He jumped inside and returned with two squares of foam. "These bodyboards are for you two, so you can catch waves easily. If you want to have a go at standing up, I'll show you later on, okay?"

Ella nodded enthusiastically. "I used to bodyboard a long time ago, I know what to do."

Richard was struggling to get the wetsuit on and dreaded the thought of having to climb out of it again.

Once suited, Yama asked them to sit with him in the sand. "Look at the beach, look at the sand, unblemished, un-ruined. By midday it will wear the scars of the impressions of feet trampling all over it, ours being the first to do harm. At the end of the day, the beach will show its damage of litter, holes dug, and the many feet that will have walked over each other. What you see now will be ruined. Every day we, like the beach, are born again. The tide will come in and wash away the ruin and evidence returning it to flawless, only for the same to happen. Every day is a beginning, a chance to be born again."

Ella's hand reached and took her father's. She smiled knowing he understood the lesson Yama told.

"Do you know why surfing not golf, Richard?"

"Because you wanted to see how stupid I looked in a wetsuit?"

"Partly. But golf is manmade. All that land to play with a ball that is about three inches across is stupid and it is so expensive, it seems vulgar. It's manmade, you can play whenever you like, there is no harmony to it."

"I wouldn't say there is no harmony to it, you're outdoors, and getting your swing right is a harmonious thing."

"Look at those waves, Richard. They have travelled for thousands of miles, over oceans, the children of massive storms, just to end upon this beach here. You can't make them come, you have to wait. Sometimes weeks, months even, the tide and weather affect where you go to ride them. This isn't a manicured lawn and planted trees, this landscape is the result of nature for a millennia. And surfing is not taking away, modifying what is there, it is enjoying it. It can be hard though, if you don't listen to the waves. Tell me what you see, Richard."

"Waves."

"What are they doing?"

"Breaking."

"If you were just to try and paddle out, those waves will keep pushing you back. You will battle with something you have not the slightest chance of winning. But if you look properly, you will see the waves break from right to left, every one does. So if you enter the sea on the left-hand side, you can paddle around the waves, in calm water and get to where the unbroken waves are. It is a longer journey but one without battle, you will get to where you want to be. What I am saying is sometimes you have to stop fighting, Richard, if you look hard enough you will see the problem and how to avoid it."

Richard laughed at the simple beauty of the metaphor. But his heart ached for the short time he had. *Make every moment count,* he thought.

"Are we going surfing or just talking?"

Richard was last in the sea. He stood as foam washed over his naked feet, fizzed and excavated the sand from around it. He wondered if he wasn't running out of time and feeling everything, would he ever have noticed how beautiful it felt. The waves were small and he took his time paddling out to the unbroken waves. Ella laughed wildly as she sped past prone and chased by the white of a wave.

Up ahead Yama paddled for a bigger wave and sprung to his feet, seeming to glide across the open wall of the wave. It was like a slow-motion dance. He turned back in a sweeping arc, back to where he came from, then pivoted the board so that it returned again toward Richard. Yama stepped foot over foot, arching his back with both feet over the nose of the board. Effortless. The wave passed by and he watched Yama from behind the wave as it finished its epic journey.

Richard sat amongst the waves, slightly out of breath, but oddly excited. He paddled for the next, but couldn't catch it. Behind it was a bigger one. *Too big,* he thought.

"Go, Dad, goooo!" Ella screamed, red-faced and elated.

The wave built, Richard paddled. As the wave stood it

seemed to take him skyward with it, and when ready it let him go. Richard surfed down the face of the wave as a rush of adrenalin hit.

"Lean to your right, lean to your right," Yama sat on his board and yelled.

Richard leaned as best he could. The board turned and began to rise up the unbroken face. It was like flying, the speed seemed unbelievable. Once at the peak of the wave he catapulted down the face again. For the first time since a child he was screaming with joy. Ella then pearled into the ocean and surfaced also laughing.

They played in the waves for hours. Yama paddled his board and sat beside Richard.

"This is brilliant. Such fun."

"I know," Yama said, "You know, all this was here, a half hour from your home all along, while you were chasing women and money."

"Look, I get it. I do. But what is the point in such when what time I have is limited?"

"Live in the moment, Richard. Share what matters with who matters, for however much time you have left. Remember when I said the best thing you ever made were memories? Well you are making them now, good ones. In the end that is all that really matters."

Yama paddled off to catch more waves, leaving Richard to wonder again what could Yama, or Gabriel or whatever he was called could be?

* * *

Once back at the van, Ella had packed a lunch for each. They sat wrapped in towels and drank sweet flask coffee with feet buried deeply in sand.

"See," said Yama pointing at the beach, "look at it

already, trampled. Us and others, dogs and children digging have defaced it. Doesn't matter though, because like I said, it will be born again tomorrow. Every sunrise, we are born again."

Ella wrapped her arms around Yama and planted a kiss on his cheek. "Thank you. Thank you for bringing my daddy back."

Richard felt a pain so deep it was unending and unyielding. How could he let his little girl think so? Allow her to think he was back knowing he would soon go and never return. She stood, wet salt hair clinging to her face naked of make-up, looking at the ocean. He yearned for the time that was squandered and cursed the time he wouldn't have. *Death knows who I am*, he reminded himself.

It was on the return trip that Richard knew the lack of time meant he had to fight for his son. There was no rebuilding or repair without him.

Evening came and it was treasured to have spent it with his wife and daughter, but the absence of Sam grew more painful.

"I need to talk to Sam, I can't leave it like this."

"Yes, Richard, you do," Anna said, "but be prepared. He is stubborn and, well, you might need to just be prepared, that is all I am saying. There are some things that can't be fixed."

"Maybe so, but I owe it to him and myself to try."

* * *

Yama and Richard set out early morning and headed to Salcombe. Once a picturesque fishing village, now an affluent clutch of holiday homes and hotels nestled at the mouth of a combination of rivers. Winding roads ensured many a snare, halting traffic in loud horn-chorused snakes.

The delay was welcome to Richard as confrontation assuredly awaited his unwelcome arrival. Once a spot was located large enough to accommodate the van, they had a long walk to the town, each step burdened with worry. The studio Sam ran wasn't in the town, it lay further down the river, alongside the craft shops and galleries that occupied what once housed fishermen and the builders of their boats. Sam's business was easy to spot, tables sat outside and used by people that looked trendy. Two floor-standing flags waved in the breeze, stylish black with white text emblazoning *'Artography'* with simply the letter 'o' a mustard yellow. Inside, thick white cubicles offered multi-coloured Holga cameras for sale, books, art and an array of fun or stylish, if a little ironic, gifts. The walls exhibited stunning photography. The first a petrified monochromatic tree, bleached and weather-beaten, it stood alone in desolate lands below a black marbled sky. The next a monotone nude, contorted yet beautiful, the shape a mere form painted by light that fell to black in an ebony surround. Next, a screaming face of a young girl, her face ivory with vivid make-up of greens and pinks shocking the features of her eyes and mouth. But somehow – maybe it was the eyes, Richard thought – he could tell she was laughing. Below each sat a plaque that read Sam Atkinson, his mother's maiden name.

The shop was busy, people bustled and enjoyed the art. Further inside, a large monitor displayed slides of family portraits, some on white, people playing, some taken inside homes, all tasteful and well-executed.

The sound of small feet running sounded from somewhere within the room above along with the joyous screaming of children. Adult laughter would then join the playful screams, pause, and feet would thunder and children would scream again.

"A family shoot. Samuel is fantastic with kids." An assistant approached with a warm smile, a handsome man, immaculately presented. He noticed both Richard and Yama listening to the din from somewhere above. "Can I help you?"

"I need to speak to Sam," Richard replied.

The assistant quickly retreated to a counter and returned with a tablet computer, scrolling for appointments. "Name?" he asked.

"I don't have an appointment. Sorry, but it is important."

The assistant went from joyful salesman to reserved consternation. "Might I ask what your enquiry is in connection with? I might be able to help."

"I'm his father," Richard said.

The assistant instantly stiffened, congenial replaced by acrimonious. "I don't think Sam will want to speak with you. In fact, I think he will want you to leave."

"Please," Richard pressed, "there are things we need to talk about."

"Oh I know well about the *things*," the assistant said angrily. "I am Alex, Samuel's partner, you know, *life* partner, his *gay* lover."

"Oh, wow, lovely to meet you, Alex," Richard thrust out his hand to invite Alex to shake. Disarmed by the gesture and confused, Alex took the hand offered, and Richard intuitively covered it with his other hand, a warm intimation of kindness. "I'm sorry, I guess I need to speak to you too. How long have you both been together?"

Alex didn't know where to put his resolve, Richard offered no animosity, only a kind and gentle request. He expected fury if he met Sam's father, a battle he had dreaded and had distorted the size of over their long relationship. "You need to speak to me too? Sixteen years.

Sam and I, sixteen years together."

"Yes, I need to apologise to you too. I could do that now, but I think I need to talk to you both."

"I'm sorry, you did say you were Samuel's *father*?"

"Yes. Things have happened, I have a family that needs to be a family, and it won't be if you both are not in it."

"Both?" Alex recoiled in shock. "I have to be honest, I was expecting a monster. I feared for the day when I would eventually meet you. Let me get you some tea and when the photoshoot is over I will go let Sam know you are here."

Outside in the salty seaside air, Richard sat with Yama and discussed little. With each passing minute pressure built. Richard felt confident that the longer the wait for an answer the more tragic the conclusion. He watched holidaying families and longed for those days.

Eventually Alex arrived to deliver expected bad news. "I'm sorry, but Sam doesn't want to see you. So, if you could kindly finish your tea and leave."

"Can I wait for Sam?"

"Sam is very busy, Richard."

"I don't want to be a problem, Alex, but I will wait all day if I have too."

"Please, Richard, understand and respect Sam's wishes, if he wanted to talk to you he would. He wants you to leave, that means I want you to leave. If you don't I will have to call the police."

"Okay," Richard stood, "Please can you let Sam know I am sorry and I need to speak with him. And to you too, I am sorry."

They walked the narrow roads of the village, toward the bustle of tourists. Richard knew that any engagement with Sam would come at a price. A price he would have to pay to close the distance between each family member. Anna's drinking, Sam's anger and Ella's lost-and reckless lifestyle mere symptoms of damage. Time might be a healer. However, Richard knew he needed to be the catalyst for any reaction.

"What now?" Yama asked.

"We wait. I don't want a confrontation at Sam's work, I owe him more than that, but I am not prepared to give up. What he thinks, isn't what it is. I need to explain."

"Your plan is?"

"To follow them to their home, and ask again. Shout if I have too. But I need to get something first."

They continued along the pretty streets. Richard ordered a sandwich and coffee for them both. Then later, more coffee and a large cookie. When the waitress wasn't looking, Richard slipped the cookie and the saucer his cup was on inside his jacket. "Come on, let's go," he said to Yama who drowned his coffee and followed.

"You didn't have to steal the biscuit, you bought it," Yama laughed.

"It was the saucer I needed."

"Needed?" Yama asked.

"Yes, needed. My insurance for later."

* * *

Richard sat in the van, nerves already gnawing at his insides, Yama behind the wheel. Alex pulled up outside the photo studio in their old Renault and pushed the door open, engine still running and the hole in the exhaust making a loud din that amplified along the narrow street. Soon Sam left, locking the doors and checking they were secure by way of a healthy shake. He jumped into the awaiting car.

At a distance Richard and Yama followed the Renault as it threaded through the arteries of countryside. Richard felt

ever more proud of his son, his independence and the life
he had made for himself.

Their car pulled into a small and overgrown car park
occupied by similar aged and tired cars and lined with
wheelie-bins. A small mews of cottages lined along and
above the parking; five homes, each a different shade of
white, some with hanging baskets some overgrown. Sam
and Alex looked happy as they laughed, walking up steps,
Sam with a bag full of shopping, waiting for Alex to open
the door of one of the sun-bleached and overgrown white
homes. Richard jumped out of the van and searched for a
cane. Not finding one to hand, he continued on without.

He steadied himself and regained his breath. He'd had a
day to consider what to say. All words that came to mind
didn't seem to equate to enough regret and sorrow, no
matter what sequence he placed them in. He hoped love in
the face of confrontation would show him what to say. He
knocked on the door.

Laughter approached before the door opened. His
beautiful son, face alive and happy turned to one of horror
on seeing his father. Sam tried to slam the door closed but
Richard had already placed his foot in the way to prevent
the action.

"Sam, wait."

"No. You don't get to say what happens. Just fuck off,
Dad, we have nothing to discuss."

"Yes, there is, Sam. So much. I love you, you are my son.
Please."

"No. I'm not. You have no right to say that. Who the hell
do you think you are? Did Mum tell you where I live?"

"No, we followed you. Please, Sam, I am still your father.
Please. Can we talk."

"Sadly, you are my father and I wouldn't waste my
breath. Just fuck off." Sam placed his hand on his father's

chest and shoved him backward, away from the door, slamming it closed.

Richard drummed on the door again and again until Sam appeared. "Seriously, you need to fuck off before I really lose my temper."

"Sam, please, just hear what I have to say."

"Anything you have to say is twenty years too late," Sam laughed angrily. "You are nothing to me and have nothing I want to hear."

"Samuel." Richard reached out for his son's arm. Sam seeing the attempt at intimacy slapped the hand free. Anger rushed to drown reason. Lost in the moment he lashed out, striking Richard in the mouth, the punch not hard, but atrophied legs failed to absorb the impact and he fell, landing in a heap at his son's feet. "I'm not looking for forgiveness, Sam."

"Just because you don't remember, I do. I remember all of it," Sam screamed. "I remember you laughing and mocking me. I remember what you called me. I remember how you treated Mum. I...me it was who held Ella as she cried from your both fighting. Mum and I were who held Ella's hair as she was sick from booze. We collected her from police stations and took her to rehab each time, not you. I will not forgive and I do not forget." The door slammed closed.

Richard slowly returned unsteadily to his feet and returned to the van.

"Ready to go?" Yama asked.

"Not yet." Richard retrieved the cookie and the saucer. "I've something I need to do." Once more Richard climbed the steps and hammered on his son's door. On the third attempt Alex answered.

"Look, you should go. Sam isn't going to talk to you. Please, just go."

"I am, I will. Will you please do me a favour? One thing." Richard handed Alex the saucer with a cookie on it. "All I want to do is rebuild a family, and that is one that involves you, Alex. If Sam loves you, then his mother and sister will. I won't stand in the way, I will be gone. Please give Sam this and tell him to place it under his bed. He will understand. It was lovely to meet you at last, Alex." Richard then turned away from his son's house for what he knew would be the last time.

"So, ready to go?" Yama asked as Richard stepped into his seat, nursing a blooded lip.

"Yeah. Let's go."

"Want to tell me what the cookie is about?" he asked.

"You know, the only real thing my family has in common is how much I let them down, I think it is the very thing that will unite them. I have no place in their lives, Sam is right about that. The cookie is to unite them. You will see what I mean soon."

* * *

Anna was in her field again when they returned. Ella was playing with her mother's dogs. Richard sat on the lawn outside the house and watched them, his heart heavy and lungs as if vessels of shattered glass. He dragged them down as he sought out selfish excess, leaving them weary and tortured. It would have been less painful if he just left them years past. Yama was right, he saw Anna and the children as possessions, owned items not souls of love and joy. He chased away their aspirations with lies and promises he had no intention of honouring. Night after night spent with men he wanted the betterment of, women he neither knew nor loved. Cocaine and whisky were chemical substitutes for the love he left to starve at home. If only he could live again, he would cast aside all the wealth and vice he had bought.

The cookie he left Sam was an ignition of a fuse to a bomb. He trusted the fall-out would be in his family's favour but not his own. Knowing Sam as only a father knows his son, even the absent ones like himself, Sam wouldn't react to the cookie instantly. The offer would fester, Sam would build a wall of defiance yet anger would build behind, until it could no longer be contained, his rage and a reaction would result. That reaction would soon arrive.

* * *

It was evening when the exhaust announced the angry arrival of Samuel's car, skidding on the loose gravel as it stopped at speed.

"Is that Sam?" Anna worried.

Richard's heart stopped the instant the car growled to a halt. He stood, ready for his ending.

"Don't believe a word that lying bastard says!" Sam screamed, the door hammering into the wall as it opened, and with force enough for a print to tumble to the floor. "He is lying, he remembers everything."

"Sam, we need to talk," Richard moved to cover the ground between his son and the remainder of his family.

"There is nothing you can say to me that can't be said in front of them. He is lying to you, he remembers every-thing."

"Richard," Anna now stood. "Is this true? You are lying? Tell me Sam is mistaken."

"He is a manipulating bastard, a lying manipulating, same as he always was, sly bastard." Sam slammed down the saucer with the cookie on it, remarkably neither broke.

"He gave Alex this to place under my bed."

Ella looked at the biscuit then at her brother. "A cookie? I don't understand?"

"When I was young, younger than you would remember, I used to get nightmares, bad ones, that there was a monster in the wardrobe. He said that nothing, not me, Mum or even monsters could resist a chocolate chip cookie, so he used to put one on a plate under my bed. If it was still there when I went to bed or when I woke, there couldn't be a monster in my room." The recollection calmed him and stirred a deep loss, one ignored since childhood.

"Samuel, I never meant to turn into the monster you feared. I need to explain."

"You were a bully, you were always trying to tough me up, *'man up'* you'd say, *'stop being a sissy'*, you hated having a gay son and you never, not for one minute let me forget. I was never good enough was I? Your disappointing *gay* son."

Richard walked around the table, Sam backed away. "No, Sam, it wasn't like that, not at all. I loved you and I wanted to protect you, that's all. It's not that I didn't want you to be gay, I didn't want you to be openly gay, so...camp."

"It is the same thing! I am who I am and that should have been enough," Sam screamed.

"It was. It is. I was wrong, I see that now."

"Do you know what I was going to bring as my item? The thing Yama asked us to bring? A tube of antiseptic cream, but then I realised the memory was mine not yours. Kids at school knew I was gay before I did, before I knew what gay was and they were cruel. I remember the bullies. Each time they pushed me to the floor, I remember you running out of the house, my dad. You were my hero, you'd chase the bad away and scoop me up in your big arms and carry me inside, and rub cream into the hurts. You'd tell me I was perfect as I was and to never change. Do you remember that?"

"Yes, Sam, but…" Richard was consumed by pain, the memory once lost, but now returned, so clear, so painful.

"But *WHAT* dad? You became them, name calling and emotional torture."

"I just wanted to protect you, Sam, that's all. The people I worked with, they were mean, cruel. I saw that the world was like them, Sam, like the bullies at your school and I couldn't change them, I just wanted to protect you from it. I loved you Sam, gay or otherwise, but I knew I couldn't protect you for ever."

"So what? You became the enemy? You were supposed to fight for me, Dad. You were my hero and you left." Sam crumbled. The pain he had been withholding for so long couldn't be contained any longer, tears fell, he became distraught. "You left me to fend for myself. She would sleep all day and I'd have to go through her purse for money and go to the shops to feed Ella and myself and suffer all the horrible names."

"Sam, I didn't know," Richard pleaded. He stepped toward his son.

"Don't fucking touch me." Sam backed further away. "You didn't know because you weren't there, you'd never come home." Sam now crippled with grief.

Ella ran to her brother and gave him the comfort that as children only they shared. "You bastard!" she screamed. "Is this a game to you? That you could just lie your way to a new start? I hate you. I feel stupid for ever wanting to believe you had changed."

Anna slapped him, then again harder leaving a stinging tattoo of red on his face. "Get out. You have ruined my family once, I have just got them back and I will not let you ruin them again."

"Anna, I need to explain."

"No. You gave up that right." Anna opened her door and stood beside it. "Leave."

Richard walked out into the chill air of a late May evening, knowing that his family were now and once again united. He didn't need harmony for his place with them as he was soon to be gone.

Yama joined him outside, silent for a moment. Richard in an ocean of joy and regret at the same time. He repaired them, uniting them using the only thing they all hated in equal measure.

"Yama, can we go back to that beach?"

"Yes," he replied.

* * *

The van once more wound through the tendrils of road within the countryside. Inside they remained silent. Richard wondered if Yama was hearing his thoughts now and didn't mind if he was. He felt no shame in the gesture he made. Now he was a responsible parent providing for them a life without the shadow of his ruination.

The moon was full and pretending to be the sun, reflecting its light onto the waves that were still arriving to end at the shore. He took his jacket and wrapped it tightly around himself and considered for the first time, here would be his end. He served no further purpose and was ready for death. He took one last look at the beautiful blue moon and hoped he had undone the mess he had made of his family. He knew he couldn't help them further.

"Yama, I'm ready."

"For what?"

"To go, die, for you to collect. I have done all that I can, and now you can take me. And thank you, Yama, for giving me time."

"Oh, Richard, I didn't come for you."

The shock of the words that came from Yama struck Richard in his stomach and stole his breath. Confused, he thought he had heard him wrongly. "What?"

Yama turned to look at Richard,

"I didn't come for you."

"What the fuck are you talking about?" Richard quickened to anger, he stood looking down on Yama and demanded an explanation. "You said I was going to die."

"No, Richard. You asked me if you were going to die, and I said yes. Everyone dies Richard, *eventually.*"

"I...I don't understand. Why are you here?"

"Because you asked for my help. We helped each other, Richard. Do you remember who was in your room when we first spoke? I was there for one of them. I have come for Ella, your daughter."

The words needed moments to sink in, Richard heard them perfectly well, yet denial battled with their understanding. Fear and anger surfaced, followed by a desperate searching grief. "No. *No."* Richard screamed at the stars. "Stop playing around. What the fuck are you talking about?"

"I have come for Ella. You got what you want, your family again."

"You bastard, I will not let you harm my little girl. No way, I won't let you. I will kill you first."

"Richard, I am taking Ella. Tonight."

"NO!" Richard screamed. His world undone, he could feel the size of his love, how his little girl needed her father, she too young and vibrant to die. "You said you were here for me." Tears fell, warmed by anger and loss. "I will not let you take my daughter."

"Jesus Christ, you fucking people. Honestly, you think you are so important don't you? You think you get to choose? You are all so sanctimonious, 'save me, save me', what is it that makes you think you get a choice? That your lives are so important?"

"You're an angel, you're meant to help people, help us, she is just a girl, she has done nothing wrong." Richard snatched at the shirt Yama was wearing and pulled aggressively, but he felt immovable, like a mountain.

"I keep telling you, Richard, I am not an angel. There are no angels." Yama stood, brushing the sand from his legs. "It is you lot that call us angels. Every time we are seen, you think we are here to save you, why? Have we ever said that? No, we haven't. Whenever death is witnessed we are there, because we take the life, not save it. I told you my name, Gabriel, Michael, Samael, Azrael, Yama. You had plenty of time to look me up, others have. Some call us angels of death, it is what I am here for, it is what I do. I have to collect, Richard, but I never said I came to collect you."

Richard lunged. Yama remained solid. Richard spilled to the sand and wailed, thundered his fist down. "She is my baby, please."

"You lot, you are so pathetic with your religions, killing each other in the name of the same God that you have given different names. To us it's funny, you elect a man as a pope who holds a solid gold cross in his hand and then tells the poor to feed the starving. You're all crazy. You all think you are so important, think your life has a purpose. It's hilarious and sickening."

"Yama, please, she doesn't deserve any harm, why her?"

"Mine isn't to question why, Richard, I just do as I am told."

Richard threw himself at Yama's feet. With his soul, he

begged for reason, for a pardon, "She is so young, why?"

"Because of you. It's your fault Richard. Ella will be so upset at your lies and how you tried to fool your family. Depressed, she will drink a bottle of wine by herself, smoke cannabis and take Valium. She will fall asleep while taking a bath and drown."

"You know her, you like her, she is like the sunshine, Yama. Don't take her, please."

"Like I said, there are checks and balances. I am sorry for you, Richard, I am. But I have to take someone."

Richard sobbed and begged in muttered tones, guttural and lost.

"If it makes it any easier, it won't be a painful passing."

"I can't let this be. It isn't fair."

"Life isn't," Yama said.

"Take me," Richard stood. "Please, you said you need someone, take me. Let me give up my life. She doesn't deserve this, I do. I've squandered my life."

"Maybe they want Ella because she is good, have you considered that?"

"Please, Yama. Let me take her place. If I kill myself, right here, right now, will that settle the debt?"

"It doesn't work like that," Yama replied. "You would give up your life for your daughter?"

"Yes. I was prepared to give my life for all of them. I was ready to go."

Yama stood, looking at the heavens, the moon painting all silver. "Listen, Richard, if I do this, if I let you take her place, you cannot back out, do you understand what I am saying? I am not saying you shouldn't or that you can't change your mind. If I can trade you for her, I will collect on you. You cannot avoid it. Do you understand?"

"Yes. I understand. I want to take her place. With all my heart."

Yama turned to face Richard. "You are a good father, Richard. Shame it took you so long and now it is too late. This is what is going to happen. To ensure your daughter's safety, I will return to your home. Before this I will drop you where you will meet your ending."

"Do I have time to say goodbye?" he asked.

"I'm sorry, Richard, no, you don't."

"Okay."

"The road that leads to town, at 11.42 tonight there will be a speeding car, the driver drunk. This is how you will die. You will be on the road and will get struck by that car. It has to be credible. The police will say you were walking to the town after a family argument. Things have to reconcile, checks and balances and all that. Do you understand?"

"Will it hurt?" Richard asked.

"Does that matter?"

"Not really. I would suffer any pain for my family."

* * *

Cloud blanketed the moon, allowing the night to become darker than dark. Richard felt like he couldn't awaken from a nightmare of being lost in a cave that offered no exit and that it waited to become his tomb. Grey light would shine through gaps in the cloud and hint at the cold landscape that soon eclipsed to black again. Languidly he pushed along the road without a destination, waiting for his ending. He thought about his daughter, her laughter and her wild abandon. Why settle for less than your heart desires when all it wants is freedom? He had amassed enough for her to flutter on like the wayward butterflies in Anna's field. He wished her to fly on and remain aimless. He cried into the opaque endless night. He knew Anna too would be better with his passing. He was a shadow on her life and she would surely blossom now. And Sam, he had every right to hate his father, but he hoped time would be gentle on his memory and that he might one day come to peace on his father's misguided love. Either way, he had no place in this world, so he pressed on into nothingness.

Occasionally rivers of light would spill over the land, searching the black as cars approached. Each time Richard looked at his watch to see if it was his time. Yet it was too early to die. The cars, slow and responsible, would crawl past and on into the empty night.

11.30.

Richard watched the minutes expire. He wished to share one more moment with his family, cherishing their memories, keeping their faces to the fore of his mind. Another car passed, its lights beacons searching. Richard placed his hands into the pockets of his jacket, he discovered thick folded paper. In the black it was hard to see as he unfolded, but what he discovered by the light of his phone was the photograph that sat on his bedside table. Him with his young happy family. Tears fell.

11.36.

Richard could walk no further. He sat on the verge sightless and blind. No more tears, only acceptance that he would soon only exist as memories.

11.40.

Richard stood. The night silent, the time was now. He walked to the tarmac and lay upon it. He didn't want anything to prevent the car from hitting him. He didn't want the driver to see him and swerve. He shut his eyes and smiled.

'You love your daughter don't you?' The voice returned.

"Very much," Richard said. "I would die for any of them a thousand times."

'Goodbye Richard.'

He looked at his watch, the time 11.41. Light was approaching, blinding white, he closed his eyes and screamed, "FOR LOVE!"

Pressure pulsed over him, a giant breath of warm.

He lay there on the road for a time. Nothing.

He checked his watch, 11.51. He was alive and there was not a car with its lights telling its arrival as far as he could see. A sense of deep foreboding coursed through him. No angel of death would make such a mistake. The night became claustrophobic, and his heart raced. Ella was to drown because of the family fight that Yama coerced to happen. He was collecting her. Yama tricked him so he couldn't keep her safe.

"NO!" Richard screamed, tearing at the stars. He ran the miles to what was once his home. His wasted muscles protested, lungs feeble, but in spite of the pain he ran through the blackness, cursing every step.

He saw the strobing blue lights dance off the trees before he saw the ambulance outside the house. Anna outside hysterical. A paramedic trying to calm her. From inside the house, fluorescent jackets carried a covered body, into the waiting vehicle with crackling radios.

Too late.

Anna saw him, alone in the darkness looking on at the dead, distraught.

"Oh, Richard, something terrible has happened."

He embraced her, deep sobs thundered from within. "I know, I'm sorry."

"He fell asleep in the bath." She turned away from the ambulance. "It's so awful."

"He?"

"Yes, Yama's dead. He said he didn't usually drink, but he was angry that things didn't work out. He fell asleep in the bath and drowned. He was so young, it's so awful."

Yama's words echoed in Richard's thoughts, *'Checks and balances, someone has to die.'*

Ella came to the door. "I'm so sorry, Dad, are you okay?" She held out her hands and joined them in embrace. His baby, his little girl. Of all the useless things he had bought to buy instead of love, his love was what gave her a second chance. "I love you both, you know that don't you." Through sniffs and sobs Ella nodded. Samuel walked outside, he held a clipboard that he returned to a medic, Alex behind him. He noticed Richard woven in embrace with his family. Sam walked to join them.

"Dad, I was angry."

"It's fine," Richard said pulling him close, "I will be there for you in your every waking breath. I promise."

The folded picture fell to the floor as Sam joined the embrace. Richard bent and retrieved it. He could see it now he wasn't in blackness; his young family and smiles. In the amber glow that spilled out from the house, Richard saw the inscription on the back written in scribbled pen.

'Live in the moment, you never know how long you have. Yama.'

PERFECT
EDGE
BOOKS

"There are many who dare not kill themselves for fear of what the neighbours will say," Cyril Connolly wrote, and we believe he was right.

Perfect Edge seeks books that take on the crippling fear of other people, the question of what's correct and normal, of how life works, of what art is.

Our authors disagree with each other; their styles vary as widely as their concerns. What matters is the will to create books that won't be easy to assimilate. We take risks, not for the sake of risk-taking, but for the things that might come out of it.